Dad's New
Shopping Trolley

First published in 2009
by Wayland

Text copyright © Jill Atkins
Illustration copyright © Eleftheria-Garyfallia Leftheri

Wayland
338 Euston Road
London NW1 3BH

Wayland Australia
Level 17/207 Kent Street
Sydney, NSW 2000

The rights of Jill Atkins to be identified as the Author and
Eleftheria-Garyfallia Leftheri to be identified as the Illustrator of this Work have been
asserted by them in accordance with the Copyright, Designs and Patents Act, 1988.

Series Editor: Louise John
Editor: Katie Powell
Cover design: Paul Cherrill
Design: D.R.ink
Consultants: Shirley Bickler

A CIP catalogue record for this book is available from the British Library.

ISBN 9780750258036

Printed in China

Wayland is a division of Hachette Children's Books,
an Hachette UK company
www.hachette.co.uk

Dad's New Shopping Trolley

Written by Jill Atkins
Illustrated by
Eleftheria-Garyfallia Leftheri

WAYLAND

Bella and Charlie went shopping with Dad.

"I hate shopping," said Bella.

"Me, too," said Dad. "The trolleys always have wonky wheels."

On the way home, they visited
Mad Uncle Albert.
"We've been shopping," said
Bella.

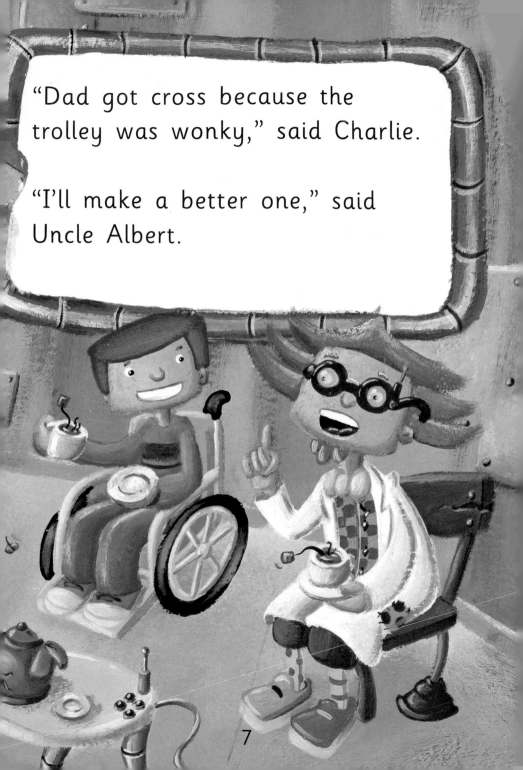

"Dad got cross because the trolley was wonky," said Charlie.

"I'll make a better one," said Uncle Albert.

The next day, Uncle Albert came round with the new shopping trolley. It had lots of long arms and big hands.

"All you have to do is wind it up,"
he said.

They all went to the shops.

"I can't wait to try this out," said Dad. He turned the key.

Shop and Spend

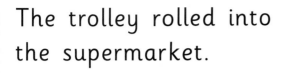

The trolley rolled into
the supermarket.

"Hooray!" shouted Charlie.
"Its wheels aren't wonky!"

Dad pushed the brake and the trolley stopped.

He pushed the button. A hand grabbed a tin of beans.

"This is perfect!" Dad cried.

The hands grabbed everything
Dad wanted.

But the trolley wouldn't stop.

A hand grabbed a box of eggs.

"No, thank you," said Dad.
"We don't need eggs."

Another hand grabbed some
ice cream.
"Watch out!" laughed Bella.

The ice cream landed next to
Mum's foot.

The arms went faster and faster. The hands took things Dad didn't want. They put things he **did** want back on the shelf.

19

Dad was beginning to get cross. Suddenly, the trolley zoomed off around the supermarket.

Everyone was laughing and pointing.

Bella and Charlie went after it.

"Albert!" shouted Mum.
"Do something!"

But Mad Uncle Albert could not
stop the trolley.

The manager ran towards them.

"Do you think he's going be very cross?" laughed Charlie.

"Stop making this mess!" shouted the manager.

At last, the trolley stopped.

"Get that trolley out of my supermarket!" shouted the manager.

"Wait! I can fix it," said Mad
Uncle Albert.

Uncle Albert got out his screwdriver and fixed the trolley.

It began to put things back where they belonged.

"It would make a great shelf filler," said Uncle Albert.

"But who will clean up this mess?" said the manager.